Shirt 6
Shorts 2
~~Dr~~
Dress 2
Sock's 2
Gliter 1
Pant's 1
Shoes 3
tennis Shoes 1
Chancletas 1
Money / realy $7800   spected $300,000
Under Word 6
Bag

The Storybook Based on the Movie

Random House New York

Columbia Pictures Presents
A Ray Stark Production
A John Huston Film

Annie

Executive Producer Joe Layton
Director of Photography Richard Moore
Choreography by Arlene Phillips
Screenplay by Carol Sobieski
Produced by Ray Stark
Directed by John Huston

Storybook Adaptation by Amy Ehrlich

The stage play *Annie* was originally presented on the New York stage by Mike Nichols. Produced on the New York stage by Irwin Meyer, Stephen R. Friedman, and Lewis Allen. Book of the stage play by Thomas Meehan. Music of the stage play by Charles Strouse. Lyrics of the stage play by Martin Charnin.

 Published in the United States by Random House, Inc., New York, and simultaneously in Canada by Random House of Canada Limited, Toronto.

Manufactured in the United States of America

Miss Farrell
Daddy Warbucks'
private secretary

Annie
A spunky 10-year-old orphan who
is searching for her parents

Daddy Warbucks
A grouchy, lonely billionaire

**Rooster Hannigan
and Lily St. Regis**
Miss Hannigan's jailbird
brother and his dim-witted
girl friend

Miss Hannigan
The mean woman who runs
the Hudson Street Orphanage

Sandy
The stray dog who
wins Annie's heart

Punjab
Daddy Warbucks'
Indian bodyguard

President and Mrs. Roosevelt
Annie's greatest heroes

The Hudson Street Orphans
The girls who live at the
orphanage with Annie

It was a hot summer night in New York City. No breeze stirred. Downtown on Hudson Street the pool halls and pawnshops were closed up tight. Sirens screamed in the distance and car horns honked. A radio on the next block played a sad tune.

High in an upstairs window of the Hudson Street Orphanage sat a young girl with a mop of red curls. Her name was Annie. For the past three nights she'd been feeding a stray dog. Now she was waiting to see if he'd come back again. Annie looked into the orphanage yard, where she'd left him bread and water. Broken glass lay everywhere, and trash had blown up against the fence. But Annie hardly noticed. This was the only home she'd ever known.

When she was just a baby, Annie's parents had left her on the orphanage steps, wrapped in a newspaper. Around her neck was a broken locket. Annie knew the note it held by heart: "Take care of Annie, our darling baby. We'll come back as soon as we can, bringing the other half of the locket so that she'll know us."

That was ten years ago. But Annie was sure her parents would show up any day. And if they couldn't get there, she planned to find them. She might

live in an orphanage, but she was not like the other orphans. As far as Annie was concerned, she was just waiting around, looking for a chance to escape.

But in the meantime a person had to keep busy. There were the younger orphans to take care of. They really *were* orphans, and they needed her. And now there was the old dog who'd been coming around. He wasn't much to look at, that was for sure. His fur was matted and dirty, and he was covered with battle scars. But there was something about him that Annie admired. He had spunk. He was on his own, a stray like she was, and come to think of it, they were both making out.

At last! The dog was coming. He was walking right toward the table she'd made from old coffee cans. There! He was eating the food, bolting it down like gangbusters. He licked his chops and looked up at her. Annie could have sworn he was smiling. "We'll try to do it again tomorrow, fella," she whispered. "If worse comes to worse, that is, and I'm still stuck here."

It was time to get down from the window sill. Miss Hannigan, who ran the orphanage, sometimes inspected late at night. She'd like nothing better than to catch Annie out of bed. The girl slid to the floor, graceful as a cat. As she tiptoed into the dormitory where all the orphans slept, she heard Molly, the youngest, crying softly.

"Molly, shut up!" It was Pepper's voice. At thirteen Pepper was the oldest girl in the orphanage and mean as vinegar.

Annie threw her a nasty look and went to Molly's bed to comfort her. A nightmare must have woken the little girl. It had happened before. Annie laid a soothing hand on Molly's forehead. "The old dog's outside, Molly," she whispered.

She could feel Molly quiver as she tried to control her tears. "Blow," Annie instructed, holding a handkerchief to her face.

Obediently Molly blew, but it sounded more like a foghorn. The other orphans stirred in their beds. "How'm I supposed to get any sleep around here?" bellowed Pepper. That did it. Now everyone was wide awake. Annie would have liked to punch her.

"Oh my goodness, oh my goodness!" said Tessie, sounding worried as usual.

Pepper began stomping around, kicking at the saggy iron cots. "Molly shouldn't be in this room. She's a baby, she cries all the time, she wets the bed—"

Molly became indignant. "I do not!" she protested.

"Ssssh," said Annie, trying to quiet her.

In the narrow dormitory room, the battle was heating up.

"Miss Hannigan's going to come in here."

"We're going to get in trouble," lisped July.

"So shut up," Pepper yelled.

"Oh my goodness, oh my goodness," moaned Tessie.

Pepper whirled on her. "Oh, blow it up your old wazoo!"

Annie had heard enough. She pulled Molly away and hoisted her up onto the window sill. "Look, Molly. Down there," she whispered, pointing.

Below in the yard the old dog gazed up at them. Then he wagged his tail and disappeared around the corner of the building. Molly smiled at Annie and gave her a hug. Then she noticed. "You got your shoes on, Annie." Her eyes filled with tears again. "I want you to stay here."

"But I gotta find my folks, Molly. They're out there somewhere, I know they are."

"Read me your note from the locket. Please?" Molly pleaded.

"Please *don't,*" said Pepper, loud and clear.

Annie didn't even bother to answer Pepper. She had more important things to think about right now. For weeks she'd been planning to run away to look for her parents. Tonight seemed as good a time as any.

"You've heard it enough," she told Molly, patting her hair. Then, as softly as she could, she jimmied the window lock, avoiding Molly's eyes. Maybe after she was settled with her parents, they could come back to the orphanage and adopt Molly as a younger sister.

"'Bye," she whispered to Molly, and pushed the creaky window open.

Carefully Annie climbed along the brickwork until she reached the fire escape. This was the hardest part. She'd have to pass right by Miss Hannigan's window. If she got caught.... But Annie didn't want to think about that possibility.

As she tiptoed by, Annie caught a glimpse of Miss Hannigan. She was propped up against her satin Coney Island souvenir pillows, drinking something clear out of a glass. Annie knew it was definitely not water. Gin, more likely. Maybe Miss Hannigan would be too drunk to see clearly. Her attention seemed to be completely absorbed in a radio soap opera. But just as Annie was about to make it around the corner, Miss Hannigan reached out the window and yanked her inside.

Annie was scared stiff, but she tried not to show it. Miss Hannigan marched her over to the closet and threw open the door. Annie gasped as she saw the switches and whips, the handcuffs and paddles, hanging there.

"I love you, Miss Hannigan," she said in desperation. Sometimes saying it could calm Miss Hannigan down.

But not tonight. Very deliberately Miss Hannigan selected a large paddle from her punishment collection.

"Touch me with that and my father'll slit your gullet," Annie threatened, raising her chin a notch.

"You don't have a father, you dirty rotten orphan," Miss Hannigan sneered.

"I do too!" yelled Annie. "And a mother. And they're coming for me."

Miss Hannigan grabbed one of Annie's pigtails and pulled the child to her. Annie gasped in pain. "This is the last time you're going to run away. I'm going to polish your backside so it

shines like the top of the Chrysler Building."

The beating was bad. When the other orphans heard about it the next morning, they were all very angry. But what could they do? Miss Hannigan ruled with an iron hand, and woe to those who crossed her. Only Annie felt defiant. She wasn't going to let Miss Hannigan stop her from running away! While the orphans got their ragged sheets ready for the laundry, Annie jumped into the laundry basket and hid there. Molly burst into tears.

"She'll put you in the cellar with the ghosts," Duffy warned. "You'll get whipped again."

"I'm gonna tell," threatened Pepper.

"Try it," said Annie, "and I'll rearrange your teeth."

Just then Miss Hannigan bustled in and grabbed the laundry basket, heading for the door. "What are you standing around for?" she screeched. "You have to do the kitchen and the bathroom before lunch, and if you skip the corners, there will *be* no lunch."

All the orphans groaned, and Miss Hannigan turned on them. "What was that I heard?"

"Nothing, Miss Hannigan. We love you, Miss Hannigan," came a chorus of voices.

"Wonderful," she said. "Where's Annie?"

Inside the laundry basket, Annie froze.

"She had to go to the bathroom," said Molly. Good for her! Annie relaxed.

Suddenly the doorbell rang loudly. "Oh!" cried Miss Hannigan. "It must be Mr. Bundles to pick up the laundry." She nearly danced to the door to open it, pulling the laundry basket along with her. Everyone knew that when there was a man around, Miss Hannigan turned all starry-eyed and giggly. A missing orphan would be the last thing on her mind. Now all Annie had to do was to keep her mouth shut and her fingers crossed.

Miss Hannigan moved in close to the middle-aged laundry man. "You're

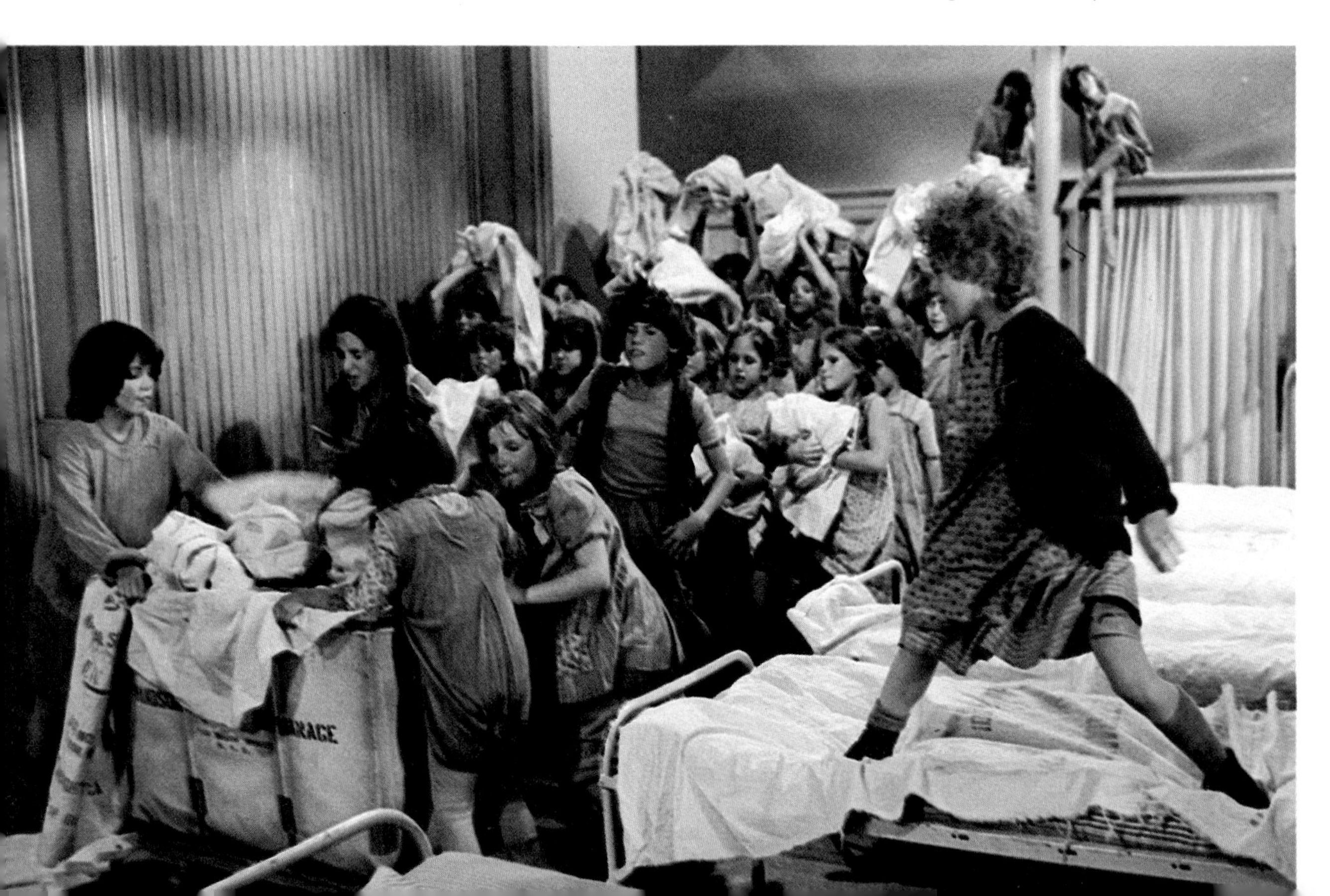

certainly looking bright and bushy-tailed today, Mr. Bundles," she said flirtatiously.

Just then Duffy leaped down the steps and began pulling the laundry basket toward the ramp into Mr. Bundles' truck.

"What're you doing out here, Duffy?" said Miss Hannigan, angry at being interrupted.

"Helping you," said Duffy. "The basket's heavy today." She elbowed Mr. Bundles, frantically hoping he'd get the message.

As he pushed the heavy basket up into the truck, a look of understanding passed across Mr. Bundles' face.

"Lemme see that basket," said Miss Hannigan suspiciously.

It was then that Mr. Bundles made the supreme sacrifice. To distract Miss Hannigan, he took her in his arms and kissed her. "Till next time, Miss Hannigan," he said gallantly.

As Miss Hannigan swooned against a lamppost like a lovesick cat and the orphans watched from the window, Mr. Bundles' truck pulled away with Annie safely inside. She poked her head up through the sheets. "Juju beans! I made it!" she said fervently.

When they got to Mr. Bundles' storefront laundry, he opened the back of the truck and fished Annie out of the basket.

"Good-bye, good-bye, Mr. Bundles. And thank you," said Annie. She hugged him gratefully, then took off down the crowded sidewalk as fast as her legs could carry her.

Drunk with freedom, she wove her way past men selling pigeons, racks of used clothes, piles of furniture. There were children everywhere—pitching pennies, playing stickball, dashing in and out of an open fire hydrant. But Annie wasn't even tempted to stop and watch. She had only one thing on her mind: to find her parents, and the sooner the better. But where was she going to look? Golly, New York was a big place!

Just then Annie noticed that a policeman had spotted her and was on her tail. She knew him only too well. He was lean and mean and he went by the name of Weasel. But worst of all, he liked to drink Miss Hannigan's gin and capture her runaway orphans.

She ducked into an alley to shake

him. Suddenly she heard a loud yelp of pain. Annie couldn't believe her eyes. There at the end of the alleyway was the old dog she'd been feeding—surrounded by nine or ten boys who were tying a string of tin cans to his tail. The boys all looked tough and were bigger than she was, but Annie didn't let that stop her.

"Get away from that dog," she said, marching up to the biggest boy.

He hardly glanced her way. "Keep walking, kid," he warned. The other boys laughed loudly as the dog ran around in circles, biting at the cans clattering behind him.

Annie was furious. They had some nerve, picking on an animal who couldn't fight back! She grabbed the leader by the arm and held on tight. "What's that dog ever done to you?"

"You want a fat lip?" he asked menacingly. It was the invitation Annie had been waiting for. She kicked him hard in the shins.

"Why, you little—" The boy lowered his head and plunged toward her.

Annie stopped him with a left to the jaw. As he reeled back against a building, she followed it with a sharp right to the stomach. The boy slid to the ground in a heap.

"Anybody else?" she called out, fists in position and eyes flashing. The other boys slowly backed off, muttering among themselves.

Very gently Annie untied the string of cans from the old dog's tail. He seemed to be all right, but he hung his head and refused to move. Annie knew how he felt. Sometimes it was hard to bounce back after you'd been mistreated. She sighed and pulled his scruffy head onto her lap. "C'mon, pal, cheer up," she said to him. "Things could be a whole lot worse."

The old dog thumped his tail once on the ground. It wasn't much, but at least it was a start. Annie headed back to the main street. By now Weasel must have given up on her. Uh oh, the old dog seemed to be following her. This would never work; he'd only slow her down.

"I can't find my own home. You can't expect me to find yours too," she told him. "Dumb dog, latch on to someone who can feed you. Give you a bath. Put something on those cuts. Go on now."

Instead he sat down at Annie's feet and gave her his paw. People were watching curiously. She leaned closer to him. "You are embarrassing me," she hissed. "Now scram." She began to race through the crowd, trying to lose him. But the dog galloped after her with surprising speed.

Then, out of the corner of her eye, Annie saw a truck from the dog pound and a man reaching out to clamp a collar around the dog's neck. Annie knew all about the pound. They took dogs there and ground them up into hamburger. That's what Pepper said, anyway.

She screeched to a stop and raced back to the pound truck. "Hey, mister!" she yelled. "You can't take that dog. He's mine."

"Oh, yeah?" said the man. "Then where's his license? Where's his leash?" He opened up the back of the truck and started to shove the dog inside.

"Please, mister," Annie pleaded, "I swear he's my dog. Cross my heart and hope to die."

The man's eyes narrowed. "All right. What's his name?"

"The dog's name?" said Annie, stalling for time. "Uh...his name's Sandy. Right. Sandy."

"Go over there and call him then," said the man, loosening the rope he'd tied to the collar.

"You mean by his name?" Annie gulped and moved off down the block. It was the noon hour. The street was crowded with workers on their lunch breaks. Shopkeepers leaned up against their plate-glass windows, and housewives strolled along holding market baskets. Suddenly it seemed to Annie that they were all staring straight at her.

"Sandy! Here, Sandy!" she said without much hope. Oh, why had she ever gotten herself into this? Annie had half a mind to go away and leave the dog to his fate. But then she remembered what it felt like to be locked up and frightened. "Come on, Sandy! Come on!" she called with new determination.

A hot dog vendor who'd been watching laughed. "Here, Rover!" he said, louder than Annie.

A toothless old woman across the street joined in too. "Rin Tin Tin! Come to Mama, Rin Tin Tin!"

The dog cocked his ears and looked from the hot dog vendor to the old woman in confusion.

Desperate now, Annie cupped her hands to her mouth and called out at the top of her lungs, "San-dy!" It was the dog's last chance and he took it. He ran straight through the crowd and right up to Annie.

"Good old Sandy!" she crowed as he jumped up and began licking her face.

The man from the pound grudgingly unlocked the collar. "All right. Guess you got yourself a dog, kid. Now go home and get him a collar and a leash."

"Yes, *sir*!" said Annie. Before he could change his mind, she raced away with Sandy bounding along at her heels. Oh, well, it looked like she was stuck with him. She sure hoped her mother and father liked animals.

But Annie's dreams of freedom did not last long. All of a sudden Weasel darted from an alley and grabbed her. Sandy nipped at the policeman's heels, but he shook the dog off easily. Then he took Annie by the scruff of the neck and marched her back to the orphanage.

Miss Hannigan opened the door. Her eyes lit up when she saw Weasel. "Oh, there's my little peach fuzz! I was worried sick. What can I ever do to thank you for saving her?" she said to the policeman. She shoved Annie aside and moved in closer to flirt with Weasel. At that moment Sandy slipped into the orphanage through an open basement window. Annie's heart raced with joy. Miss Hannigan had not noticed him! Sandy was safe!

As soon as it was dark she tiptoed downstairs to get him. Sandy spent the night under the covers with her. Curled up next to the dog's warm body, Annie felt safe and peaceful and happier than she could ever remember.

In the morning she decided to introduce Sandy to the other orphans while they were sewing in the sweatshop.

"Oh my goodness, oh my goodness!" exclaimed Tessie.

"His eyes are pretty," said Kate.

"He's filthy. Plus he smells," Pepper said, holding her nose.

But Sandy was not insulted. He licked Pepper's face and wagged his tail happily.

Suddenly the door burst open. There stood Miss Hannigan. Her fists were clenched and her footsteps echoed as she marched across the room. Even Annie was terrified. She covered Sandy with a bedspread and sat down at her sewing machine. But it was too late.

Miss Hannigan reached down and dragged Sandy out by his tail. "This goes to the sausage factory. And you're going to the cellar."

Annie gasped. Not the cellar! It was full of spiders and rats and strange noises. In the cellar she'd be locked in the dark, unable to help Sandy. Tears sprung to her eyes.

Just then the doorbell rang. Miss Hannigan tightened her grip on Annie. Then she opened the door.

The young woman who stood outside was prettier than anyone Annie had ever seen. Her face was delicate and her clothing was beautiful. Annie could tell right away that she was a real lady.

"How do you do, Miss Hannigan. I'm Grace Farrell." Her voice, like the rest of her, was perfect.

"Hold it, sister," screeched Miss Hannigan. "If you're selling beauty products, I don't need none."

"Beauty products? I'm afraid I don't know what you're talking about." Miss Farrell came in and sat down. "Actually, Miss Hannigan, I'm the private secretary to Oliver Warbucks."

Miss Hannigan let go of Annie in surprise. "Do you mean the Oliver Warbucks that has more do-re-mi than all the Rockefellers put together? Oliver Warbucks the millionaire?"

"No," Miss Farrell corrected her, "Oliver Warbucks the billionaire. You see, Miss Hannigan, Mr. Warbucks wants me to invite an orphan to spend a week in his home. He's sent me here to select one."

Annie could not believe her luck. She'd heard about Oliver Warbucks on the radio and had seen his name in the newspapers. This was a golden opportunity, the chance of a lifetime. She stepped into the middle of the room and pointed to herself. Then she gave Miss Farrell her cutest, most appealing smile. The young woman gasped, surprised to see her there. Then her eyes met Annie's. Some deep current of understanding seemed to pass between them. Annie smiled again, and this time her smile was real. Beneath Miss Farrell's efficient manner Annie sensed a soft, gentle woman, like the mother she'd so often imagined.

But Miss Hannigan had no intention of letting Annie spend a week with a billionaire. She shoved the girl behind her. "Wonderful idea," she said. "What sort of orphan did Mr. Warbucks have in mind?"

"Well, friendly and intelligent. And, of course, happy," said Miss Farrell.

At that Annie burst into laughter, kicking her feet into the air.

"You're asking for it, my little prune pit," said Miss Hannigan. She picked Annie up and threw her into the paddle closet. "Now, Miss Farrell, let's get down to business. How old an orphan would you like?"

"Oh, the age doesn't matter. Seven or eight—"

Annie opened the closet door a crack and signaled to Miss Farrell, holding out ten fingers to show how old she was.

"Actually," said Miss Farrell, "I think a ten-year-old would be perfect. And Mr. Warbucks did say he wanted a red-headed child."

Annie slid out of the closet grinning. Then she shook Miss Farrell's hand. "Hi," she said. "I'm Annie."

"Hold it," said Miss Hannigan. "Not so fast. You can't have Annie. She's—she's a drunk."

To Annie's great relief, Miss Farrell

just laughed. "Fiddle-faddle. I think you had better let me take her. Your boss, Mr. Donatelli, happens to be a great personal friend of Oliver Warbucks'. If I were to tell him about this ...well, let's just say you wouldn't want to lose your job."

Miss Hannigan thrust Annie savagely at Miss Farrell. "Go ahead then. The brat's yours."

"Come along, dear," said Miss Farrell, straightening Annie's skirt. "Mr. Warbucks' limousine is waiting."

Annie imagined the days ahead. Eating good food, sleeping in a soft bed, walking down marble halls with Sandy by her side. Sandy! She had forgotten all about him. She stopped in her tracks and grabbed Miss Farrell's arm. "My dog! We have to take Sandy. He's really nice, really really good. He never jumps on people."

Hearing his name, Sandy got up and immediately jumped on Miss Farrell. He licked her face a mile a minute.

"I'm afraid not, Annie," Miss Farrell said. "He's very sweet. But Mr. Warbucks—"

Annie sat down on the floor and said stubbornly, "Then I'm not coming."

Miss Farrell looked at her, astonished. She was beginning to discover what everyone who knew Annie learned sooner or later: this sweet, fragile looking little girl had a will of steel.

"If we leave Sandy, Miss Hannigan's gonna send him to the sausage factory," Annie whispered.

"All right." Miss Farrell glared at Miss Hannigan. "We'll take the dog."

"Leapin' lizards!" exclaimed Annie. She ran down the orphanage steps without a backward glance. But when she saw the enormous limousine parked outside, she stopped short and her mouth dropped open. A dangerous looking Oriental, dressed in a chauffeur's uniform, opened the back door with a bow. All the orphans who were leaning out the upstairs windows cheered wildly.

"Don't go, Annie!" Molly called as the car's engine began to purr.

"Don't worry. I'll be back. I'll bring everybody presents. Good-bye, good-bye. Wish me luck!"

Boy, am I ever going to need it! thought Annie when the car pulled up a short time later before a building the size of a museum.

Before Miss Farrell could ring the bell, the door was opened by the most gigantic man Annie had ever seen. He was an Indian, wearing a turban pinned with a ruby the size of a walnut. Sandy bared his teeth and growled.

"Annie, meet Punjab," said Miss Farrell. Then she pointed to the Oriental chauffeur who hovered nearby, trying to control Sandy. "And that is The Asp. Punjab and The Asp are Mr. Warbucks' bodyguards."

"Wow!" said Annie with awe in her voice. She walked over to Punjab and took his hand. "I sure wouldn't want to come across *you* in a dark alley."

Miss Farrell laughed and led Annie inside. "Come along now. Let's get you settled."

Annie looked around. The place was not exactly what you could call

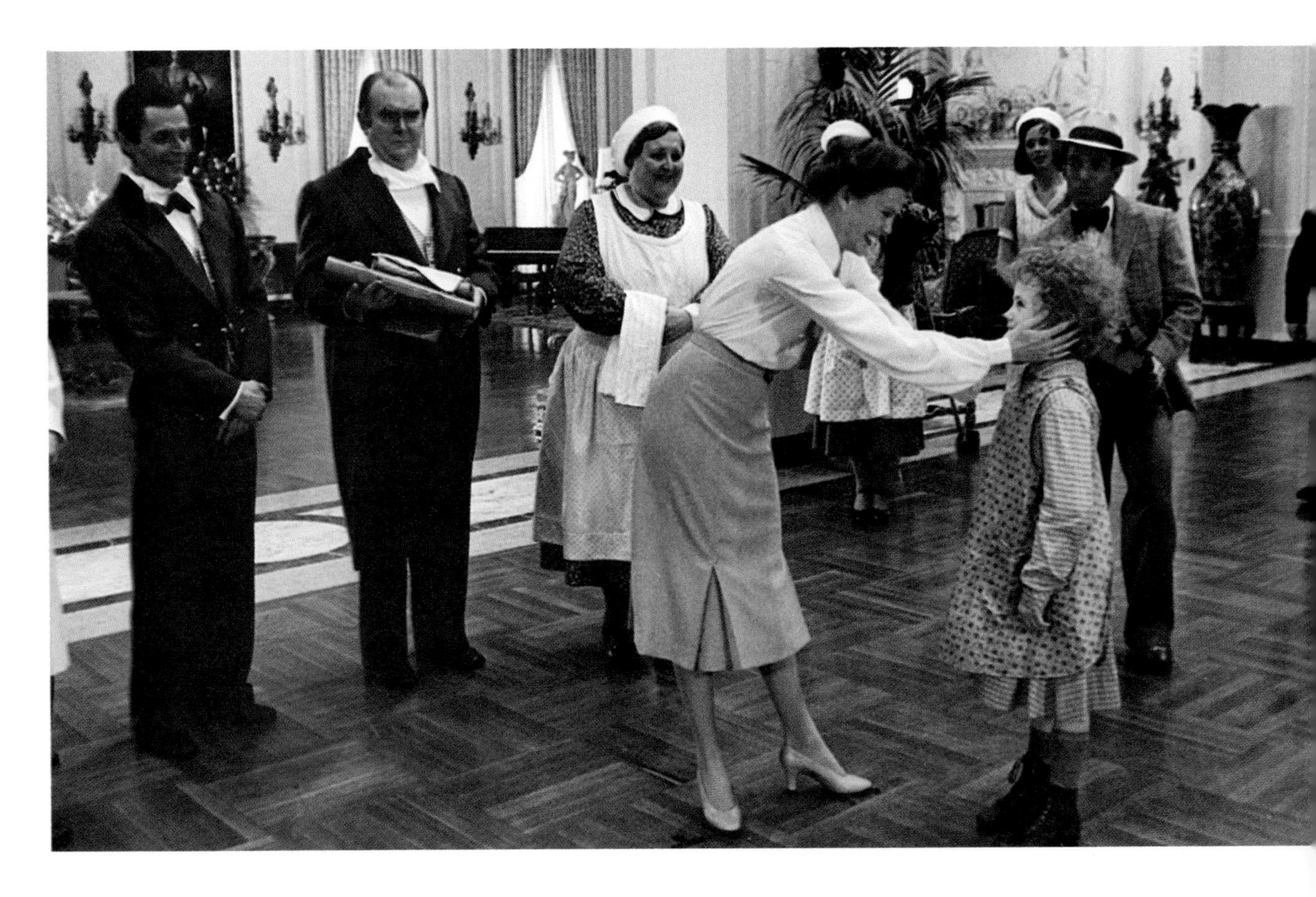

cozy, she thought. The ceiling above her head was hung with tinkling crystal chandeliers. The highly waxed floor was big enough for a skating rink. Servants were everywhere. There was even a photographer waiting for them, ready to take pictures. Where did she fit in? Annie had never felt smaller and shabbier. She glanced down at her dress. Why had she never noticed before how ragged it was?

Miss Farrell pulled a bellcord. Instantly all the servants stood at attention. "Is everything ready for Mr. Warbucks' arrival?"

"Yes, Miss Farrell," came a chorus of voices.

"Good. I have an announcement for everyone. This is Annie and her dog, Sandy. They'll be staying with us for a week."

Annie's eye widened as all the maids curtsied.

"Now, Annie, what would you like to do first?" asked Miss Farrell.

Annie looked around the vast living room. Then she began to roll up her sleeves. "The windows, I guess. And after that the floors. Do you have any ammonia?"

All the servants laughed. But Miss Farrell hugged her tightly. "Oh, Annie, you won't have to do any cleaning while you're here. You don't have to earn your keep. You're our *guest*."

She began to lead Annie on a tour of the house, and the servants fell into step behind them. Annie's head was swimming. Each room was more magnificent than the last. Paintings glowed from the walls, and deep carpets muffled their footsteps. Now that she understood she was welcome here, Annie began to enjoy the wonders of this new world. The servants really were kind. They fussed about whether she would sleep on silk sheets or satin ones, and they even asked her if she

wanted her baths plain or with bubbles! It was wonderful to be treated this way by grownups. At the orphanage the most Annie had ever hoped for was to avoid a beating.

From the living room and the library, they went to the indoor swimming pool. Here Annie could contain her joy no longer. Throwing out her arms wide enough to embrace them all, she crowed, "Oh, boy! I think I'm gonna like it here."

Sandy chose that exact moment to plunge into the pool. Dirt streamed from his fur into the shimmering turquoise water. Three maids ran for towels; the butler jumped back in horror.

Suddenly the sound of sirens split the air. Hurriedly the servants began to straighten their uniforms and polish their buttons. The sirens became even louder. The noise was deafening. Then suddenly all was silent. Bewildered, Annie turned to Miss Farrell.

"It's Mr. Warbucks," she said. "Don't be afraid, now." But Annie could not help noticing that Miss Farrell's voice shook. What was there about Oliver Warbucks that made them all so fearful?

"To the living room," said Miss Farrell. "Let's go."

The first thing Annie noticed about Oliver Warbucks was his speed. She had never seen anyone move faster. He swept through the door and stormed across the room. Miss Farrell quickly handed him a glass of brandy and a Havana cigar. "Welcome home, sir," she said.

A note in her voice caught Annie's attention. Miss Farrell sounded as if she were actually glad to see him. Her cheeks were shining and her eyes danced with affection.

But Oliver Warbucks did not appear to notice. "Well, what's been going on around here? Any messages?"

Miss Farrell pulled out a small notebook, instantly becoming the world's most efficient private secretary. "President Roosevelt called three times this morning. Said it was urgent."

"Phooey. Everything's urgent to a Democrat," said Mr. Warbucks. "What else?"

"Mr. Rockefeller, Mr. DuPont, Mr. Vanderbilt, Mr. Carnegie."

The names were all familiar to Annie. They belonged to some of the most powerful men in the world. She peeked out from behind a pillar where she'd been hiding. *What about me?* she thought. *When's he going to ask about me?*

Mr. Warbucks picked up his briefcase and headed for the stairs. Miss Farrell rushed after him. "I'd like you to meet—" she began. Annie's heart thumped. This was it!

But before Miss Farrell could say another word, Oliver Warbucks bumped right into Annie. Both of them landed on the floor. As he glared at her the photographer leaped up and took their picture.

"What the devil is going on here?" roared Mr. Warbucks.

Miss Farrell came to the rescue. "This is Annie. Remember, sir? The orphan who'll be staying with us for a week? Public relations..." She lowered her voice and began to whisper, but Annie was able to hear most of what she was saying.

It soon became clear that Mr. Warbucks hadn't really wanted an orphan in his house at all, much less a girl orphan. Annie was confused and hurt. For a moment she wanted to run away, out the back door. But she had no idea where it was.

Miss Farrell began pleading with Oliver Warbucks to let Annie stay. It was the first time in Annie's life that anyone had defended her. Suddenly she was filled with new determination. She wouldn't let him send her back to the orphanage. She would stay here all week. And somehow she would make Oliver Warbucks like her.

Back at the orphanage Miss Hannigan was drowning her troubles in a tall glass of gin. It wasn't fair. How come a no-good kid like Annie was living in the lap of luxury while she was still stuck in this dump?

Suddenly a loud crowing sound interrupted her black thoughts. Miss Hannigan whirled around. Uh oh, it was her younger brother, Rooster. They must've let him out of jail early. Rooster was trouble. He'd been in and out of jail at least a dozen times. The only time he ever showed up at her place was when he needed money.

"Rooster, what a surprise," she said sarcastically.

"Hi, Sis," said Rooster with an oily smile. "I want you to meet a friend of mine, Lily St. Regis."

"Very pleased to meet'cha," said Rooster's girl friend. She filled a glass with gin and began to paw through Miss Hannigan's jewelry.

Miss Hannigan was in no mood for either of them. "Get outa here, Rooster, and take her with you."

Rooster grabbed her arm threateningly. He and Lily had seen Oliver Warbucks' limousine leaving the orphanage. They smelled cash, lots of it, and they wanted the details.

When Miss Hannigan told Rooster that Annie would be staying at Warbucks' mansion for a week, his eyes glazed over with greed. "Maybe we can make a bundle through the little brat," he said slowly. "There's gotta be a way to fix it."

This was just what Miss Hannigan needed to hear. Maybe she'd wind up living on Easy Street after all. "If you got some scheme to get rich offa Annie, count me in," she told Rooster.

At that moment Miss Hannigan was the furthest thing from Annie's mind. She was carrying Mr. Warbucks' dinner tray to his office. It was heavy and she didn't want to drop it. If he could only see how helpful she was, maybe he would change his mind about her. She'd heard him tell Miss Farrell that he'd wanted a boy orphan. Well, she'd prove to him that girls were every bit as good—or better.

Inside Oliver Warbucks' office, phones were ringing and teletype machines were clicking away. Papers were piled everywhere. Mr. Warbucks was dictating a letter while Miss Farrell took shorthand at lightning speed.

"What are you doing here?" snapped Mr. Warbucks when he saw Annie.

"I brought your dinner." Annie crossed the room and put the tray in his lap. "I'm sorry I'm not a boy, Mr. Warbucks."

"Go to bed," he told her, not even looking up.

"But it's only six thirty," said Annie desperately. She wasn't getting anywhere with this man. What did he want, anyway? He seemed to have everything—piles of money, servants who jumped at his every command, a private secretary like Miss Farrell who obviously thought he was swell. Yet he didn't even notice. Annie's resolutions to be good and quiet and helpful were suddenly forgotten. She had to say what she really thought.

"You're a hard case, Mr. Warbucks. All these nice people doing all these nice things for you, and you don't appreciate any of it." She plunged on. "Does being rich give you the right to be horrible?"

Well, at least she had gotten his attention. Oliver Warbucks' eyes were riveted to her face. Secretly he could not help being impressed. It was the first time in twenty years that anyone had spoken to him so honestly.

"Does being an orphan give *you* the right to be horrible?" he said. But his voice was gentler than his words.

"No, sir. I'm sorry, sir."

Oliver Warbucks cut off her apology with a wave of his hand and turned to Miss Farrell. "She can stay," he said.

"Oh, boy!" yelled Annie, and leaped into Miss Farrell's arms.

It was what Annie had been waiting for. She had thought it was all she needed to make her happy. But later that night, after Miss Farrell had put her to bed, she was suddenly frightened. The room she was in seemed enormous. The wind was blowing, and the trees outside cast strange shadows across the walls. Sandy began to growl.

Maybe, thought Annie, the problem was that she was not used to sleeping in a room by herself. She decided to get up and find out if Mr. Warbucks was still awake. Sure enough, a light was on in his office.

Mr. Warbucks looked up in surprise when she walked in. "Shouldn't you be in bed?" he asked.

"Sandy was nervous. He kept growling," Annie explained. "Are you getting a lot of work done?"

"I'd get more done if Roosevelt would leave me alone. He keeps calling me up, wanting my support for his so-called New Deal. It's laughable."

President Roosevelt was one of Annie's heroes. She knew he was on the side of the poor people. In 1933 times were hard in America, and Roosevelt was trying to help by making jobs. But she didn't want to argue about that now.

Suddenly Sandy began to bark. "Do something about your dog," commanded Mr. Warbucks. Impatiently, he leaned down to grab Sandy.

At that very instant a shot rang out, shattering the window and exploding the ticker tape machine. Mr. Warbucks had missed being killed only because of Sandy's barking.

With a hunter's reflexes, Sandy vaulted through the broken window after the gunman. Later Annie learned that her dog had held the man at bay until Punjab and The Asp had come to

tie him up. Sandy was a hero!

"It's really been quite a day," Miss Farrell said later as she tucked Annie in for the second time that night.

Annie nodded. Her mind was already on something else. She had seen how Miss Farrell had rushed to Mr. Warbucks' side as soon as the shot was fired. She had seen the concern in her eyes. Annie was certain that Miss Farrell was in love with Oliver Warbucks. She wondered what she could do to help.

Early the next morning she began a campaign to get Mr. Warbucks to notice Miss Farrell. "You know something?" she said to him at breakfast. "It just so happens that Miss Farrell thinks you're the greatest thing since sliced bread. Meantime she does all the work around here and you don't even know her first name."

"I do. It's Grace," said Mr. Warbucks, heading toward his office. "Now if you'll excuse me, Annie, I need to get to work." He closed the door firmly.

If there was one thing Annie loved, it was a challenge. Finally she realized that she herself held the key. Miss Farrell liked her, and now Mr. Warbucks liked her too. All she had to do was bring the two of them together in a romantic setting and then arrange to vanish....

That night Annie suggested taking in a movie at Radio City Music Hall. It would be perfect. Miss Farrell would get all dressed up, and he'd see just how gorgeous she was. They could even hold hands in the darkness of the theater. But Annie soon discovered that Mr. Warbucks was not planning to come.

"Then I don't wanna go either," she said firmly.

"Come now," Oliver Warbucks said. "You may think Miss Farrell—I mean Grace—does all the work around here, but it's not entirely true.

I'm a busy man. A very, very busy man. I don't have time for movies."

"I know. That's okay. Really. I understand." Annie made her voice quiver a little.

Mr. Warbucks stared at her in dismay. He hoped she was not going to cry. He didn't think he could bear it. But when Annie glanced up quickly at him, he suddenly realized it was all an act. He had fallen for it hook, line, and sinker. The child was tougher than she looked, he thought. In fact, she reminded him a little of himself.

"I must be losing my grip," he said, sighing. "All right, Grace. There'll be three of us tonight."

When they got to Radio City Music Hall, accompanied by Punjab, The Asp, and Sandy, the giant marquee read "Sold Out." But when they went inside the vast, ornate theater, no one was there except the ushers. Organ music began to play. Annie looked around at the gilded ceilings, the red velvet curtains, the gleaming mirrors. Awed by the majesty of it all, she took Mr. Warbucks' hand. He smiled down at her, strangely moved by her gesture.

"Where is everyone else?" she asked.

"Mr. Warbucks bought up all the tickets," Miss Farrell explained. As soon as they sat down, the house lights dimmed and the curtains slowly opened. The show had begun.

Annie had never imagined it would be so beautiful. A chorus line of women in spangled costumes danced together in perfect rhythm. And Mr. Warbucks was looking at Miss Farrell as if he had never really seen her before. Annie smiled to herself in secret triumph. It was time to leave the two of them alone. She sank down into the soft velvet seat and fell fast asleep.

CITY Music Hall RADIO
"CAMILLE"
"CAMILLE"

The next morning Annie was still sleeping when Miss Farrell cornered Oliver Warbucks in the garden. "Sir, I was wondering—" she began.

He held up a hand for Miss Farrell to be quiet, intent on the ticker tape he was reading. "You know, Grace, I think I'm going to have to close the factory in Pittsburgh."

Miss Farrell could not have cared less about the factory in Pittsburgh. "It's about Annie," she said boldly. "Couldn't we keep her?"

Mr. Warbucks looked horrified. But Miss Farrell rushed on. "You haven't seen that dreadful orphanage. I can't bear to send her back there."

"Absolutely not. You should know me by now. I love money. I love power. I do not now and never will love children."

Her concern for Annie made Miss Farrell brave. This was one time Oliver Warbucks would not make her back down easily. "Watching you with her last night, I thought maybe you did care for Annie," she said, her voice rising. "Well, I guess I was wrong."

She turned to leave the garden, but Mr. Warbucks caught hold of her hand. "Wait. I just noticed something. You're very pretty when you argue with me."

Miss Farrell blushed. "Thank you, sir, but—"

"Call me Oliver," he insisted.

"Would you mind if I ask you a question, Oliver? Do you really love only money and power? They're never going to love you back."

Suddenly it seemed very quiet in the garden. Grace Farrell and Oliver Warbucks were motionless, staring into each other's eyes. Though neither of them were ready to admit it, they had just fallen in love.

"What about Annie?" Miss Farrell asked finally. "I could get the adoption papers signed this morning."

"That won't be necessary. Why don't you buy Annie a little present? That locket she always wears is broken; get her a new one from Tiffany's. I'll take care of the papers. In fact, I'll go to the orphanage myself."

A short time later a long, shiny Duesenberg drove slowly down Hudson Street. Oliver Warbucks peered out the back window. So this was where Annie had come from! He saw the ragged children sitting on the stoops and felt the defeat and sadness of the place. Suddenly Mr. Warbucks made himself a solemn vow: Never again would Annie be lonely or poor or mistreated. She was going to be his daughter.

First, however, he'd have to deal with Miss Hannigan. He had the feeling it wasn't going to be pleasant. He went to the door and rang the bell. When he told Miss Hannigan that he wanted to adopt Annie, he thought the woman was going to faint dead away.

"Will you excuse me for just a moment?" she said. Then she went into the next room and let out a bloodcurdling scream of rage.

"Are you feeling better?" Mr. Warbucks asked when she returned. "I do hope so, because I'm a busy man and I don't have all day. Your signature please, Miss Hannigan." Mr. Warbucks handed her his fountain pen with a flourish and watched carefully as she signed the adoption papers.

But in the car going home he began to get nervous. He wondered if Miss Farrell had bought the locket yet. The truth was that Oliver Warbucks was very good at taking, but the idea of giving terrified him. What if Annie didn't want the locket? What if she didn't want *him*?

When he walked into the living room, Miss Farrell was waiting. She handed him an elegantly wrapped

jeweler's box, but he threw it back at her as if it were a hot potato. "You give it to her. She likes you better than she likes me."

"Why, Oliver, I do believe you're feeling shy," teased Miss Farrell. "Now here she comes. Pull yourself together."

Annie had just returned from a karate lesson with The Asp. She came running over to Mr. Warbucks.

"Oh, hi, Mr. Warbucks. Wanna see what I learned today?" Without waiting for an answer, she clobbered him with a fast karate kick, laying him out cold on the floor.

Annie went pale. "Gee, I'm sorry. I didn't know it would work."

Instantly Miss Farrell, Punjab, and The Asp were at his side. "She didn't

know it would work," Mr. Warbucks told them. "Don't worry. I'll be fine."

"In that case I think we'll leave you two alone a minute." Miss Farrell slipped the jewelry box into his hand and left the room before he could protest.

Mr. Warbucks smiled awkwardly. "Annie, I want to talk to you about something very serious."

"You don't want me anymore, right?" she said. It had been too good to be true. He was sending her back to Miss Hannigan early.

"On the contrary, I do. Good Lord, I..." Oliver Warbucks was at a loss. He'd fought his way to the top, he'd lost and made fortunes, but this was by far the hardest thing he'd ever had to do.

He tried another approach. "Annie, can we have a man-to-man talk?"

"Sure." She settled herself in an enormous chair and looked up at him.

"You know, I was born poor, just as you were. But by the time I was twenty-one, I'd already made my first million. Making money was all I ever cared about...until now. But in the past week I've realized that no matter how many cars and houses and beautiful things I own, if I have no one...to share them with, well, I might as well be broke. Do you understand what I'm trying to say, Annie?"

"Kind of."

"Kind of?"

"I guess not."

Oliver Warbucks had run out of words. He handed her the jewelry box

and watched nervously as she lifted out the locket. "Let me put it on you," he said.

Annie's reaction took him by surprise. She jumped away as if he had hit her. "No!" she cried.

Mr. Warbucks was hurt and angry. "But you haven't even looked at it. Here; on the back it says, 'To Annie, with love from...Daddy Warbucks.'"

Annie shook her head. "No, I gotta wear my old locket! See, Mr. Warbucks, when my parents left me at the orphanage, they kept the other half so I'd know them when they came back. I'm gonna find them someday. I'm gonna have a regular mother and father like a regular kid. I am."

Annie didn't want to hurt his feelings, but she had to be honest. "You've given me so much already, Mr. Warbucks. You've been nicer to me than anybody in the whole wide world. But I've been dreaming of my folks as long as I can remember, and I just gotta find them."

Oliver Warbucks felt as if his heart were breaking. But he loved Annie and he would try to do what was right for her. If she wanted her parents and they were still alive, then by gosh, he was going to find them!

The next morning banner headlines blazed across the front pages of New York's newspapers: BILLIONAIRE OLIVER WARBUCKS OFFERS REWARD FOR ORPHAN ANNIE'S PARENTS. The police were on the case, and so was the FBI.

That evening Annie and Mr. Warbucks went on the radio to announce the search nationwide. The show was *Bert Healy's Iodent Hour,* the favorite of millions of American listeners. After the Boylan Sisters sang the famous theme song, "You're Never Fully Dressed Without a Smile," Mr. Warbucks stepped up to the microphone. "It's swell to be here in the studio tonight, Bert Healy. I am now conducting a coast-to-coast search for Annie's parents. Furthermore, tonight I am offering a reward. Fifty thousand dollars, to any couple who can prove they are the parents of the little orphan, Annie."

At the Hudson Street Orphanage, Annie's friends had sneaked into Miss Hannigan's office to listen to her radio. "Oh, boy!" said Molly as Mr. Warbucks finished his announcement. "Annie's gonna find her folks!"

Miss Hannigan had heard the show too. But for her it was more like a nightmare. First a billionaire wanted to adopt Annie, and now the rotten kid was going to be as famous as President Roosevelt. "Kill, kill!" Miss Hannigan yelled, running into her office. But the orphans had already scattered.

The following day Mr. Warbucks gave Annie the very best present yet: a trip to Washington, D.C., in his auto-copter to visit President Roosevelt. As they cruised high among the clouds in a brilliant blue sky, Annie thought that she had never been so happy in her life. "If all your dreams come true, do you die?" she asked Mr. Warbucks.

"Of course not! You live happily ever after," he said, giving her a hug.

President Roosevelt and his wife, Eleanor, served them tea at the White House. They were as fine and noble as Annie had imagined them. The only problem was that Mr. Warbucks kept arguing about Roosevelt's programs to help the poor. "If you ask me," he said, "it's all impractical foolishness. How much will the programs cost? Who's going to run them?"

President Roosevelt winked at Annie. "I was hoping you would...you and Annie," he replied.

"Leapin' lizards!" said Annie eagerly. "How can I help?"

"You could help us recruit the young people," said the President. "Many of them have given up hope. They think their government doesn't care if they live or die."

Annie knew all about hopelessness. Back in the orphanage she had fought against it every day of her life.

"Oh, Mr. Warbucks," she said, turning to him. "I'm so lucky, but think of all those other kids. We gotta help, we just gotta."

Mr. Warbucks couldn't say no to Annie. Seeing him weaken, Mrs. Roosevelt reached over to take his hand, and the President actually cheered. Without quite understanding what had hit him, Oliver Warbucks had just become a member of Roosevelt's team.

On Hudson Street, Miss Hannigan was pacing back and forth in her office. She was so angry about Annie's good fortune that she couldn't even sleep. Suddenly she heard a knock at the door.

On the steps stood a meek and raggedy couple. The woman wore a hat with a bedraggled feather on it, and the man wore a straw boater and had a mustache. "Excuse me," he said, peering at her nearsightedly. "Are you the lady who's in charge of this establishment?"

"Unfortunately," said Miss Hannigan.

"Ten years ago we left our little baby girl on the front steps. We were starving and we couldn't take care of her. But now we have a nice hardware store in New Jersey. We never wanted to leave our little girl. Do you still have her? Do you have our Annie?"

"Annie? You're Annie's parents?" said Miss Hannigan weakly.

"Our place isn't fancy but it's home," said the woman. "There's a yard out back, and we have some chickens."

"And a rooster," added the husband. He let out a loud crow and pulled off his glasses and mustache.

It was Rooster! Miss Hannigan staggered and had to hold on to the doorframe. He was her own brother, yet she never would have recognized him!

Rooster and Lily soon persuaded her that if they could fool her, they could easily fool Oliver Warbucks. They were after the reward money and they needed her help. They wanted any information Miss Hannigan had that would convince Warbucks they were really Annie's parents. In return they promised to split the money with her.

Miss Hannigan began to search the office, muttering to herself. "Years ago ...the cops came here. They told me her parents were killed in a fire. They brought me their junk. There was something—up here I think."

She climbed to the top of a rickety bookshelf and pulled out a yellowed envelope. "Eureka!" she shouted. "I have it." With a thundering crash the bookshelf collapsed.

Rooster and Lily dragged her out from under the rubble and opened the envelope. There it was—the other half of the locket. The three of them looked at each other, realizing that they held a fortune in their hands. That broken, tarnished piece of jewelry was their ticket to Easy Street.

But all along someone else had been in on their scheme. Molly was eavesdropping upstairs and had heard

every word through the bathroom drainpipe. She scrambled down and jumped onto Pepper's bed. Urgently she shook the older girl and whispered, "Pepper, wake up. They're going to do something bad to Annie! We gotta warn her."

"Y'want a knuckle sandwich, Molly?" Pepper shook her off and stuck her head under the pillow.

But Molly was not so easily discouraged. She went around the dormitory, waking up all the other orphans, telling them what she had overheard. When she explained how Miss Hannigan's friends were planning to use the locket to get the reward money, even Pepper realized they'd better do something to save Annie. And fast!

Even though it was the middle of the night, everyone at Oliver Warbucks' mansion was still awake. Miss Farrell, Punjab, and The Asp had interviewed over eight hundred couples. All of them claimed to be Annie's parents. But so far none of them had known about the locket. The living room was a shambles, and a long line of people still stretched around the block. Finally Miss Farrell sent them all home. "It seems pretty hopeless," she said, sighing. "I never realized before how many dishonest people there were in New York."

Annie burst into tears and ran to her room. It had been a long and disappointing night for her. Mr. Warbucks followed her. He walked over to the window seat where she sat and touched her hair gently.

"I guess they're dead," said Annie, not even looking at him. "I guess I've known that deep down for a long time."

"I'm not giving up. Don't you give up, Annie."

"I didn't want to be just another orphan, Mr. Warbucks. I wanted to believe I was special—"

He took her by the shoulders and forced her to look him in the eye. When he spoke, his voice sounded almost fierce. "You are special. Don't ever stop believing that, Annie."

Just then the doorbell rang. Together Mr. Warbucks and Annie wandered into the hall and looked over the bannister.

Down below they could see a meek and raggedy couple pleading with

Miss Farrell at the door. The woman wore a hat with a feather on it, and the man carried a straw boater and had a mustache. "We're Mr. and Mrs. Mudge," he was saying. "From Hoboken, New Jersey. Ten years ago we left our baby girl on the steps of the Hudson Street Orphanage, wrapped in a newspaper."

Everything suddenly stopped. Annie began to walk down the stairs as if she were in a trance. Near the front door Sandy growled softly, but no one noticed.

Just then the woman spotted Annie. She pulled on the man's arm and drew in a sharp breath. "Oh, Ralph, do you think that's our...Annie? Look, she still has the locket." She rushed across the room and fitted her half of the locket into Annie's. Then she looked her full

in the face. "Our little girl. We've finally found you."

Annie stood there, numb and confused. The parents she'd always yearned for were right there, holding out their arms to her. She knew she should have been happy, but something felt very wrong. Instinctively she turned to Mr. Warbucks, hiding her face against his chest.

"I suppose you heard about the reward on the radio?" Mr. Warbucks said suspiciously.

"What reward?" asked the man. "We don't even have a radio."

"How did you know Annie was here then?" asked Miss Farrell.

"Some dame at the orphanage told us," he said. "Look, here's her birth certificate. My wife has kept it next to her heart all these years."

Mr. Warbucks grabbed the worn piece of paper and read it. "'Ann Marie Mudge. Born October eighteenth, 1922.' Well, there doesn't seem any doubt about it. Grace, write Mr. and Mrs. Mudge a check for fifty thousand dollars."

Annie finally let go of Mr. Warbucks. She looked at the two strangers who were suddenly her parents and tried to get used to the idea. "I'll get ready," she said in a voice that was almost a whisper.

As Annie was packing, surprised by the sadness she felt when she had expected to feel only joy, the orphans too were preparing to leave. One by one they wiggled through a skylight and ran to the edge of the orphanage roof. It was a long way down. "Oh my goodness! Oh my goodness!" moaned Tessie again and again like a prayer.

With Pepper in the lead, they balanced on a narrow beam and went across the next roof. Then they dropped onto an awning and jumped to the ground. Without even looking back, they were off and running.

The city was quiet and empty. At a big square park with a wide archway they collapsed, exhausted by fear and worry. "We're never gonna make it," said Pepper. "We'll never get there in time to rescue Annie."

Just then Duffy pointed to a street sign. "Look! This is Fifth Avenue. Remember on Bert Healy's show he said they lived at nine hundred and something? We can't be too far! C'mon, let's go!" She boosted Molly onto Kate's back, and they started off again.

Block after block after block. It seemed to the orphans that they had walked miles. Finally they stopped to rest at Forty-second Street outside a library with broad steps and two enormous marble lions. "Gee, I never knew there was such a beautiful place in this crummy city," said Kate.

Pepper was fed up. "I say we go back!"

"We *can't*," said Molly.

"We've been walking for a hundred years. We're never going to get there."

"We *have* to!" said Molly. All the other orphans agreed. Pepper was outvoted.

The ragtag bunch of children continued on their way. They never noticed the old pickup truck that went by, driven by a man with a shabby straw hat and a mustache. Nor did they see the little girl who sat by his side. But someone inside the truck saw *them*. At the next red light a large shaggy dog jumped out the window and bounded over.

"Sandy!" Molly screamed. She fell on him with delight. His tail wagged frantically, and he began to lead them up Fifth Avenue in the direction of Oliver Warbucks' mansion.

Inside the truck Annie began to cry. Why had Sandy run away? He'd never left her before. Suddenly a woman leaped onto the road in front of them, waving her arms. "Rooster! Hey, Rooster!" she screamed. Annie's eyes widened in horror. It was Miss Hannigan, and they were stopping for her!

Something was very, very wrong! Annie thought of escaping, but it was too late. The woman who claimed to be her mother was holding her so tightly that she couldn't move. Miss Hannigan crawled into the pickup and slammed the door. "Step on it!" she told Rooster. "Her dirty rotten friends escaped."

Then there's still a chance! thought Annie. Maybe Sandy would lead the orphans to Mr. Warbucks. Maybe he would be able to rescue her in time. *Come on, Mr. Warbucks,* she said to herself. *You're my only hope. You've always been my only hope. Oh, if only I had known it sooner!*

It was well after two in the morning, and Oliver Warbucks sat alone in his office. He missed Annie dreadfully. Now that she was gone, his dream of happiness had ended. He gazed wistfully at the Tiffany locket he'd bought her. She'd never even tried it on. *Stop that!* he told himself. *She has her own locket and now she has her own mother and father. It's all for the best.*

With a sigh he put Annie's picture away in a drawer. Maybe if he didn't have to look at it every day, it would be easier to forget her.

Suddenly the doorbell rang. He stormed downstairs. There sat Sandy, surrounded by a bunch of poorly dressed, tired looking little girls. Punjab, The Asp, and Miss Farrell hovered nearby.

"What is the meaning of this?" Mr. Warbucks demanded.

The smallest girl stepped forward. "Sir, we're friends of Annie's—"

Oliver Warbucks cut her off. "She's gone," he said unhappily. "Her parents came and got her."

The little girl gazed up at him and shook her head. "That wasn't her parents, mister. They was bad peoples."

An older girl chimed in. "Molly heard them, your Highness. Talking to Miss Hannigan. They're gonna steal your reward money and hurt Annie. They—"

There was a moment of horrified silence. Then Punjab, The Asp, Miss Farrell, and Oliver Warbucks all swung into action. Each one rushed to a different phone while the orphans watched, wide-eyed.

"I want J. Edgar Hoover at the FBI!" shouted Mr. Warbucks. "J. Edgar, the orphan, Annie, has been kidnapped! I want every one of your men east of the Mississippi on this case within the next twenty minutes." He slammed down the phone. "Punjab, you and The Asp take the autocopter. They might be headed toward New Jersey. Come on, Grace, you're coming with me."

Mr. Warbucks' guess had been correct. At that very moment Rooster's pickup was crossing the Bayonne Bridge into New Jersey. Halfway across Rooster hit the brakes and turned to Lily. "This looks like as good a spot as any. Let's get rid of the kid."

"You mean kill her?" asked Miss Hannigan, alarmed. "You didn't say anything about killing her. That wasn't part of the deal."

"Who asked for your two cents?" said Rooster. He opened the door and got out of the pickup. Hundreds of feet below, Annie could see moonlight reflecting on the water. If Rooster pushed her off the bridge, she'd hit the water like it was concrete. In a split second Annie made her decision. She slipped out of the open door and ran for her life.

Almost immediately Rooster was upon her. He twisted her arm behind her back and lifted her onto the railing of the bridge. Annie fought him like a wild animal. "Warbucks is gonna knock your lights out! Warbucks is gonna rearrange your teeth!" she screamed, kicking at him. One of her blows made contact. As Rooster doubled over in pain, she grabbed the check from his pocket and took off.

Her heart was pounding; her legs were moving like pistons. Before her she could see the towering Manhattan skyline. But behind her the truck was revving up. She reached the end of the bridge and raced through empty cobblestone streets. Faster and faster came the pickup, closing the gap. Its headlights threw gigantic shadows against the deserted warehouses of lower Manhattan.

Annie threw a quick look behind her, then sprinted around a corner. Oh, no! She'd gone into a loading dock that ended at an open railroad bridge. There was no way out. She flattened herself against a building and heard the door to the pickup slam shut. Rooster had gotten out and was chasing her on foot. The truck backed up and began to come at her from the other direction. Annie's eyes darted around wildly. She was trapped!

In desperation she ran onto the dark and looming bridge. Rooster was gaining on her. She climbed up, using the

ties of the bridge as if they were a ladder. Higher and higher she went until she was two stories above the street. Now Annie was crying, no longer able to keep back her terror. Where was Mr. Warbucks? She knew he would try to save her, but soon it would be too late.

Suddenly Annie heard a familiar voice. It was Miss Hannigan! She was coming up the bridge after Rooster, clutching her huge purse and muttering, "Now I'll admit she's a horrible child. A dreadful, obnoxious child. But that's not enough to kill her for, Rooster, and I'm not going to let you do it."

"Get down from here, you fool," gasped Rooster. He kicked at Miss Hannigan and then lunged for Annie. All at once there was a new sound, a deafening roar from the sky. Annie looked up. Mr. Warbucks' autocopter had arrived!

It swooped in over the bridge, then turned. The door opened. Punjab tied one end of his turban to the autocopter and lowered himself down slowly. He was trying to reach Annie.

Down below, the loading dock swarmed with policemen. There were a dozen police cars, and more policemen were arriving on horseback. Sud-

denly, with a screech of rubber, the Duesenberg pulled to a stop next to the bridge. Oliver Warbucks and Miss Farrell slammed the doors and took off running. "Bring a net!" Mr. Warbucks shouted to the policemen.

But Annie was only dimly aware of all this activity. High up at the very edge of the bridge, she was struggling desperately for her life. All at once she lost her balance. Down, down, down she fell, plummeting like a stone toward the river below.

Instinctively she grabbed at a steel beam to stop her fall. Rooster rushed down the railroad ties and reached for

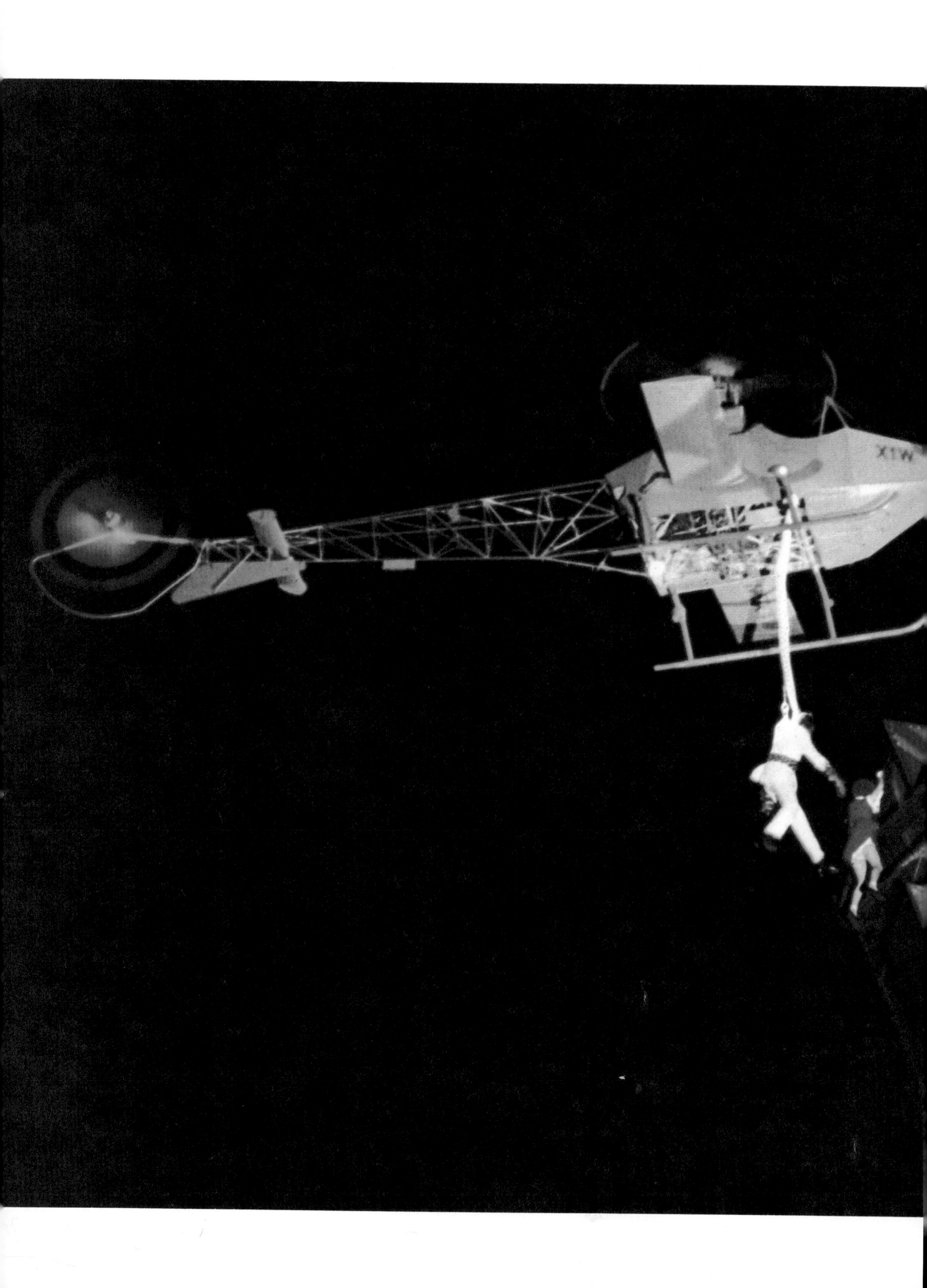

her from below. But Miss Hannigan was waiting. She slammed her huge purse down on Rooster's fingers, and he let go. Screaming, he slid down the bridge and into the net the police had strung up to catch Annie.

Now Annie dangled above the river. Her hands ached and she was out of breath. How could she hold on any longer? Then, as if in a dream, she felt Punjab's arm around her waist and heard his soothing voice. She let go of the beam and went limp in his arms. "Do not sleep yet, Princess," he told her. "You must hold on to me. I will need both hands to pull us to safety."

With her last ounce of strength Annie managed to wind her arms around Punjab's neck. Hand over hand, he hauled himself up into the autocopter while she clung to him.

Mr. Warbucks was waiting on the loading dock as the autocopter landed nearby. Annie leaped out and ran into his arms, realizing how much she had come to love him. They held each other for a long time. The police cars left, taking Rooster and Lily away. But Oliver Warbucks and Annie were aware only of each other. Never again would they allow themselves to be separated. The worst nightmare of their lives had finally ended.

The next day Oliver Warbucks threw the biggest party New York had seen in years. All the important people in business and government were invited. For Annie's sake he had even invited President Roosevelt. But the guests of honor were Annie's friends—the orphans who had saved her, and Miss Hannigan.

The garden blazed with flowers. A band was tuning up, and a small circus had been hired to perform. Clowns and jugglers strolled through the crowd; tightrope walkers balanced high in the air.

Suddenly Mr. Warbucks signaled for silence. Everyone turned expectantly as the French doors at the top of the stairs opened. There stood Annie. Her red hair was a mass of perfect curls, and she wore her prettiest red and white dress. Sandy sat beside her, embarrassed by the pink and blue ribbon around his neck. As they walked down the stairs the band began to play.

Oliver Warbucks left Miss Farrell's side and offered Annie his arm. He swung her into the first dance while the guests gathered around to watch. The orphans stood at the edge of the crowd. They were happy for their friend, yet Annie's closeness to Mr. Warbucks made them all more aware of how lonely they were. As Annie and Mr. Warbucks danced by, Molly walked toward them longingly.

"Could you maybe find some folks

for Molly?" Annie asked. "She doesn't wet the bed anymore. Ever."

"Absolutely," Mr. Warbucks said, patting Molly on the head. "I'll find homes for all your friends."

The party went on far into the night. The guests ate and drank and danced. Suddenly fireworks exploded against the dark sky. Bursts of red, white, and blue spelled out Annie's name in letters as tall as trees. The guests cheered wildly, but Annie and Mr. Warbucks were having the most wonderful time of all.

In the middle of a dance Oliver Warbucks took the gold locket from his pocket and fastened it around her neck. Annie put her arms around him.

"I love you, Daddy Warbucks," she whispered to him. "I really, really do."